by Sarah Hines
Stephens

# BACKWARD
# BOWWOW

illustrated by
Art Baltazar

Superman created by
Jerry Siegel and Joe Shuster

Picture Window Books™
a capstone imprint

# Starring...

## BIZARRO KRYPTO!

## KRYPTO
### THE SUPER-DOG!

## ACE
### THE BAT-HOUND!

## STREAKY
### THE SUPER-CAT!

## ALFRED PENNYWORTH
### BATMAN'S BUTLER!

# TABLE OF CONTENTS!

## SUPER-PET HERO FILE 001:
# KRYPTO

Heat & X-ray Vision

Super-hearing

Flight

Super-smell

Freeze Breath

Super-speed

S-shield

Super Hero Owner:
**SUPERMAN**

**Species:** Super-Dog
**Place of Birth:** Krypton
**Weakness:** Kryptonite
**Favorite Food:** Ka-pow Chow!

**Bio:** The childhood pet of the Man of Steel, Krypto the Super-Dog has the same powers as his heroic master.

## SUPER-PET ENEMY FILE 001:
# BIZARRO KRYPTO

Ice & X-ray Vision

Super-hearing

Flight

Super-smell

Flame Breath

Backward S-shield

Super-speed

**Super-villain Owner:**
# BIZARRO

**Bio:** When Krypto the Super-Dog crashed on Htrae, the Bizarros created his evil twin called Bizarro Krypto.

**Species:** Bizarro Dog

**Place of Birth:** Htrae

**Weakness:** Blue Kryptonite

**Favorite Food:** Pineapple Upside-down Cake

## Chapter 1

# BACKWARD PLANET

# SMAAAASH!

Shortly after midnight, an alien shuttle crashed down in the city of Metropolis. The strange rocket ship scraped across a mall parking lot. A trail of sparks streamed out behind it.

**SKREEECH!** The shuttle skidded to a halt next to a dumpster. A door in the side of the craft opened, and out stepped a white dog. The alien canine had a large head and red eyes. He was strong and wore a flowing red cape.

The alien looked a lot like Krypto

the Super-Dog. But he was not Krypto.

He was actually the exact opposite.

He was **Bizarro Krypto!** And he

had never meant to land on Earth.

Bizarro Krypto was the only passenger onboard a shuttle from the planet **Htrae**. The shuttle had flown far off course. It had gotten caught in the Earth's gravity.

From the space ship's window, Bizarro Krypto had watched the round planet growing closer and closer. It looked very, very different from his home planet.

EARTH

HTRAE

**"Good bumpy landing,"** said Bizarro Krypto. The alien canine climbed out of the shuttle.

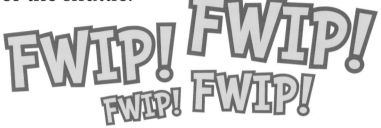

He shook himself off. Then he walked into the middle of the mall parking lot.

The moon was full. The parking lot was empty, and the stores were closed. Bizarro Krypto started to worry. On Htrae, the stores were always busy at night. Where was everyone?

Bizarro Krypto followed the sidewalk through Metropolis. He passed more closed stores. He passed more dark houses full of sleeping people.

Bizarro Krypto did not understand why people would sleep at night!

Moments later, the sun started to rise. People began to wake up. Bizarro Krypto was stunned by what he saw in the light. Peeking in windows, he saw dogs lying and eating on the floor. Humans read on couches and sat at tables.

That was not all! The more Bizarro

Krypto looked, the more confused and

worried he became. The people and

animals on this round planet were all

backward. **Nothing made any sense!**

Bizarro Krypto was about to head back to his ship. Suddenly, a man in a bathrobe opened his door nearby. A small puppy scampered out.

Bizarro Krypto stopped to watch what would happen next. The young dog picked up a newspaper and trotted back to drop it at the man's feet.

"Good dog!" said the man.

Then the owner reached down and patted his dog. He handed the pet a chew bone.

Bizarro Krypto thought it was weird for a dog to bring a newspaper to a person. On Htrae, people gave papers to dogs so they could chew them and make reading the news harder.

Still, that was not the strangest thing Bizarro Krypto saw! As he watched, the small dog took the bone. She ran off and dug a hole in the yard. **PLOP!** Then she dropped the bone in it!

Bizarro Krypto couldn't take it. **"Stop,"** he barked. **"You no do that!"**

The chew bone belonged in a frame. It was nasty and ugly and needed to be on display so all could enjoy it!

The little dog looked up, confused. "I'm saving it for later," she said shyly.

"**No, no, no!**" Bizarro Krypto said.

He didn't have time to explain what

the dog was doing wrong. She ran off

barking toward the fence.

Bizarro Krypto could not believe his

eyes. The dog was chasing after a cat!

Bizarro Krypto was more baffled than ever. What was a dog doing chasing a cat? It was like nothing he had ever seen.

Feeling a little shaken up, Bizarro Krypto walked toward downtown. **The creatures of Earth needed his help.**

# Chapter 2

# A SHOCKING DISPLAY

The people and animals of Earth were starting their day. Bizarro Krypto thought they were doing it all wrong.

He had never seen dogs wearing collars. Collars were for humans! He had never seen people walk dogs on leashes. Those were for humans, too!

Then Bizarro Krypto saw the most shocking thing of all. Through the windows at the Museum of Natural History, the alien dog spotted an enormous skeleton. It was a dinosaur skeleton, clean and shiny.

**"That not good,"** Bizarro Krypto growled. **"That not good at all."**

On Htrae, big dry bones like those had to be buried. Only meaty, stinky bones were hung up for display. Huge bones like those in the museum, without anything to chew on, were too terrifying to show to the public.

Below the enormous skeleton, people stood still and stared. Bizarro Krypto thought they were frozen in horror. He had to help them. Nobody should have to look at such awful bones!

With incredible speed, Bizarro

Krypto burst into the museum.

**WOOOOSH!**

He grasped one of the giant bones

in his jaws and flew toward the exit.

Alarms sounded. People screamed.

"They happy," he said. "I helping."

Outside, Bizarro Krypto spotted a

large grassy area. It was the city park.

**THUD!** He touched down and started

digging. Dirt flew out of the hole faster

than wind from a hurricane. **FWOOOM!**

When the hole was finished, Bizarro Krypto flew back and forth carrying bones. He'd dug a pit so huge a house could have fit inside! Soon, he would have all of the big bones hidden in it. The Earth people would be safe.

Bizarro Krypto was proud. He did not hear the sirens coming.

**WEE-OOO! WEE-OOO!**

"Stop! Police!" one of the officers shouted. Six police had formed a line to block Bizarro Krypto from going back into the museum.

Bizarro Krypto didn't stop. He flew right past the police. **WHOOSH!** They tried to catch him in a net, but it was useless against the dog's alien powers.

**"We need help!"** one of the police officers shouted.

The officer was right. The only Earth creatures with enough power to stop a Bizarro dog were a pack of Super-Pets.

One of the officers put out the call, and just in time. Inside the museum, Bizarro Krypto had begun to pull apart the skeleton of a whale.

Moments later, the real **Krypto the Super-Dog** and **Ace the Bat-Hound** arrived at the scene.

"Let's go!" Krypto barked. "That crazy dog is destroying the museum!"

"Wait," Ace cautioned. "He looks a little like you."

Krypto shook it off. "No he doesn't," he said gruffly. **"He's a bad guy. Bad guys don't look like me."**

Ace did not move. He was a good detective. He wanted to wait a moment to figure out what was happening.

Through his mask, Ace watched Bizarro Krypto flying back and forth, hauling and burying bones. He definitely did look like Krypto. But he didn't act like him.

The people at the museum had started throwing trash at the strange dog, trying to make him stop. Their attention only made him tear down the displays faster.

**"You no have to say thank you,"** Bizarro Krypto told the crowd. He ducked his head shyly. But the people didn't understand him.

Bizarro Krypto thought they were being nice. On Htrae, throwing trash was a way to show how much you liked something.

Ace didn't know this. **All he knew was that something was very wrong.**

**"Come on! Let's stop this pooch already,"** Krypto said.

"We can give it a shot," Ace agreed. "But there's more going on here than meets the eye."

Krypto had no idea what his friend was talking about. The Super-Dog stepped out to block the Bizarro's path. Krypto unleashed a blast of icy breath to stop this backward dog in his tracks.

Bizarro Krypto dropped his bone. Then he fired a warm blast of his own. The two streams of air met, creating a swirling vortex. **It was a standoff!**

While Krypto and his reverse twin were busy, Ace moved. He snagged the stolen bone and dragged it back toward the museum. The crowd that had gathered gave him a loud cheer.

Bizarro Krypto caught on. He sent one last blast of hot breath at Krypto and turned to face the Bat-Hound.

**FWOOOOOSH!**

**"Bad dog,"** Bizarro Krypto barked at the Super-Pet. **"You frighten poor people. Bad."**

The backward bowwow grabbed the bone back, snatching it easily. Then he flew toward the giant hole he'd dug.

"I helping," said Bizarro Krypto.

"**Helping?**" Ace repeated the word to himself. "**Bad dog.**"

Then Ace remembered something. Batman had told him about **Bizarro World** once. His crime-fighting partner had explained that the **Bizarros** were different from earthlings. Their world was the exact opposite of Earth.

The trouble was, their ways made no sense here. Batman had also explained to Ace that because the Bizarros were just as strong and powerful as Earth's super heroes, they were extremely hard to control. Their ideas could be harmful even if they meant well.

If this other Krypto was a Bizarro from Htrae, the best thing the Super-Pets could do would be to send him home. **But how?**

# Chapter 3

## NONSENSE

"**Krypto!**" Ace called to his friend. "Keep an eye on Bizarro. I'll be back."

Without stopping to explain, Ace took off. He had to find whatever had brought Bizarro Krypto to Earth. They were going to need it to send the backward bowwow home again.

Krypto watched Ace running down the street. He was not sure what the other dog was doing, but he knew Ace liked to have a plan. He also knew that Ace's plans were usually good.

All Krypto needed to worry about was his odd opposite. Drawing a deep breath, he turned and tried again to freeze Bizarro Krypto in his tracks. Bizarro Krypto fought back with fiery breath. **FWOOOOOM!**

*Oh well,* Krypto thought. *If I can't stop him, at least I can keep him busy.*

Krypto was drawing a big breath when he picked up a new sound with his sensitive ears. It was the soothing purr of a cat.

**"Streaky!"** shouted the Super-Dog.

Krypto was relieved that another Super-Pet was coming to join him, but he was not sure Streaky would be much help.

**Supergirl's orange cat** did not leave his home often. He liked to nap during the day and fight crime at night. Still, it was a good thing he had answered the call.

The Super-Dog was just about to deliver one more chilly gust when he saw Bizarro Krypto **freeze in his tracks.**

# WHUMP!

Streaky landed beside the Super-Dog. **"What's the problem?"** he asked, casually licking his paw.

Krypto didn't answer. He was staring at Bizarro Krypto.

The alien dog still had not moved. His eyes were wide. He tried to blow out another hot breath, but coughed and staggered backward instead.

He was afraid of something, and that something had to be Streaky!

Krypto had seen dogs that were afraid of Streaky before, but usually not until the cat revealed his powers. Bizarro Krypto was freaked out before Streaky had done a thing.

**"He's afraid of cats!"** Krypto said aloud, trying not to laugh.

**"Then this should be fun,"** Streaky purred. **"Where do we want him?"**

"Away from the museum," Krypto answered.

Streaky flew right at Bizarro Krypto. The frightened dog launched himself at top speed. He fled toward the clouds. The real Krypto and Streaky flew after him. They had him on the run!

"This is purrfect," Streaky shouted to Krypto. He flexed his claws. "But what should we do now?"

Krypto sniffed the air. Ace was nearby. He pricked up his ears — Ace was calling to them!

"Chase him this way," Krypto said.

Streaky picked up the pace and chased Bizarro Krypto in the new direction. In moments, they were in the parking lot where Bizarro Krypto had crash-landed.

Ace was there with Alfred, Batman's butler. Alfred had a way with gadgets. He was tinkering with Bizarro Krypto's spaceship.

**"There you are, sir,"** Alfred said to Ace. He gave the silver craft a pat. **"All ready to go."**

Ace barked up to the Super-Pets flying overhead. Streaky and Krypto knew just what to do. Bizarro Krypto knew what to do, too! He flew to his ship and scrambled aboard.

Using his nose, Bizarro Krypto pushed the button that sealed the hatch. He prepared for take-off.

**"Nothing make sense here,"** the odd dog muttered to himself as he took off. Earthlings were beyond help.

Watching from the ground, the Super-Pets were happy to see Bizarro Krypto go. He may have meant well, but he would be better off on his own square planet, where everything made complete nonsense.

**END!**

# KNOW YOUR HERO PETS!

1. Krypto
2. Streaky
3. Beppo
4. Comet
5. Ace
6. Robin Robin
7. Jumpa
8. Whatzit
9. Storm
10. Topo
11. Ark
12. Hoppy
13. Batcow
14. Big Ted
15. Proty
16. Gleek
17. Paw Pooch
18. Bull Dog
19. Chameleon Collie
20. Hot Dog
21. Tail Terrier
22. Tusky Husky
23. Mammoth Mutt
24. Dawg
25. B'dg
26. Stripezoid
27. Zallion
28. Ribitz
29. Bzzd
30. Gratch
31. Buzzoo
32. Fossfur
33. Zhoomp
34. Eeny

 1

 2

 3

 4

 5

 6

 7

 8

 9

 10

 11

 12

 13

 14

 15

 16

 17

 18

 19

 20

 21

 22

 23

 24

 25

 26

 27

 28

 29

 30

 31

 32

33

34

# KNOW YOUR VILLAIN PETS!

1

2

3

4

5

6

7

8

9

10

11

12

13

14

15

16

17

18

19

20

21

22

23

24

25

26

27

28

29

30

31

32

33

34

# AW YEAH, JOKES!

What do you call a really cold dog?

What?

A pupsicle!

What kind of dog likes to take baths?

Not sure.

A shampoodle!

What do dogs like to eat for breakfast?

I give up.

Pooched eggs!

# WORD POWER!

**attention** (uh-TEN-shuhn)—focus or concentration on something

**earthling** (URTH-ling)—a being from planet Earth

**gravity** (GRAV-uh-tee)—the force that pulls things down toward the surface of Earth

**hurricane** (HUR-uh-kane)—a storm with high winds that starts in the ocean

**museum** (myoo-ZEE-uhm)—a place where interesting objects of art, history, and science are displayed

**sensitive** (SEN-suh-tiv)—able to react to the slightest change

**vortex** (VOHR-teks)—a swirling whirlpool of water or air

# MEET THE AUTHOR!

## Sarah Hines Stephens

Sarah Hines Stephens has authored more than 60 books for children and written about all kinds of characters, from Jedi to princesses. When she is not writing, gardening, or saving the world by teaching about recycling, Sarah enjoys spending time with her heroic husband, two kids, and super friends.

# MEET THE ILLUSTRATOR!

## Eisner Award-winner Art Baltazar

Art Baltazar is a cartoonist machine from the heart of Chicago! He defines cartoons and comics not only as an art style, but as a way of life. Currently, Art is the creative force behind *The New York Times* best-selling, Eisner Award-winning, DC Comics series Tiny Titans, and the co-writer for *Billy Batson and the Magic of SHAZAM!* Art is living the dream! He draws comics and never has to leave the house. He lives with his lovely wife, Rose, big boy Sonny, little boy Gordon, and little girl Audrey. Right on!

# READ THEM ALL!

# DC SUPER-PETS!

# THE FUN DOESN'T STOP HERE!

## Discover more:

- **Videos & Contests!**
- **Games & Puzzles!**
- **Heroes & Villains!**
- **Authors & Illustrators!**

# @ www.capstonekids.com

Find cool websites and more books like this one
at www.facthound.com Just type in Book I.D.
9781404864801 and you're ready to go!

## Picture Window Books™

Published in 2013
A Capstone Imprint
1710 Roe Crest Drive
North Mankato, MN 56003
www.capstonepub.com

Cataloging-in-Publication Data is available
at the Library of Congress website.
ISBN: 978-1-4048-6480-1 (library binding)
ISBN: 978-1-4048-6845-8 (paperback)

Summary: When Bizarro Krypto crash lands
on Earth, he can't believe his eyes. Humans
own dogs as pets! On his planet, everything
is the exact opposite — canines rule the
world! Before returning home, he promises
to make things right . . . or maybe wrong.

Art Director & Designer: Bob Lentz
Editor: Donald Lemke
Creative Director: Heather Kindseth
Editorial Director: Michael Dahl

Printed in the United States of America
in North Mankato, Minnesota.
032016   009601R